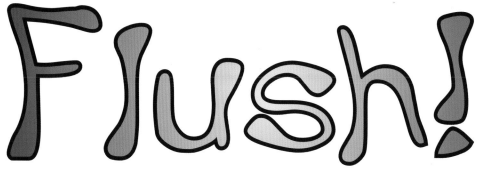

Flush!

an ode to toilets

By Charlie Williams

Sound Safari Theater

Flush! an ode to toilets

Text and illustration copyright © 2006 by Charlie Williams
http://www.soundsafaritheater.com
Seattle, WA

Continuity Checker: Ima Wiggins
Art Chimp: J. Tarner
Speling and grammaticalry-ness: Pat Duke
Kevin and Lisa: Thanks for sharing
Motivational Instructor: Linda Wheeler
Color Designs: Dr. Melody A. Williams
Sporting Supporters: Kylie and C.J.
Guinea Pigs: Tale Traders
Porpoise Handler: Adolph N. Trainer
Party Planner: Tom Foolery
Continuity Checker: Ima Wiggins

Summary: A boy takes a rhyming rest room tour, showing the sounds of a variety of toilets. For ages 3 and up, but feel free to actually decide for yourself.

ISBN 0-9772870-0-9

[1. Toilets- juvenile poetry. 2. Noise- juvenile poetry. 3. Flush- juvenile poetry. 4. Onomatopoeia- juvenile poetry. 5. Potty humor- fiction.]
1. Williams, Charlie, ill. 2. Title

First edition special director's-cut printing, 2005
1 2 3 4 tell the people what she wore.
2000-0 -0 party over, whoops, out of time.

Printed in China

Dedicated to Mel, Ky, and C's.
-C.W.

WHIRL and SWIRL

is a wondrous, joyful delight!

makes me
shiver and cower!

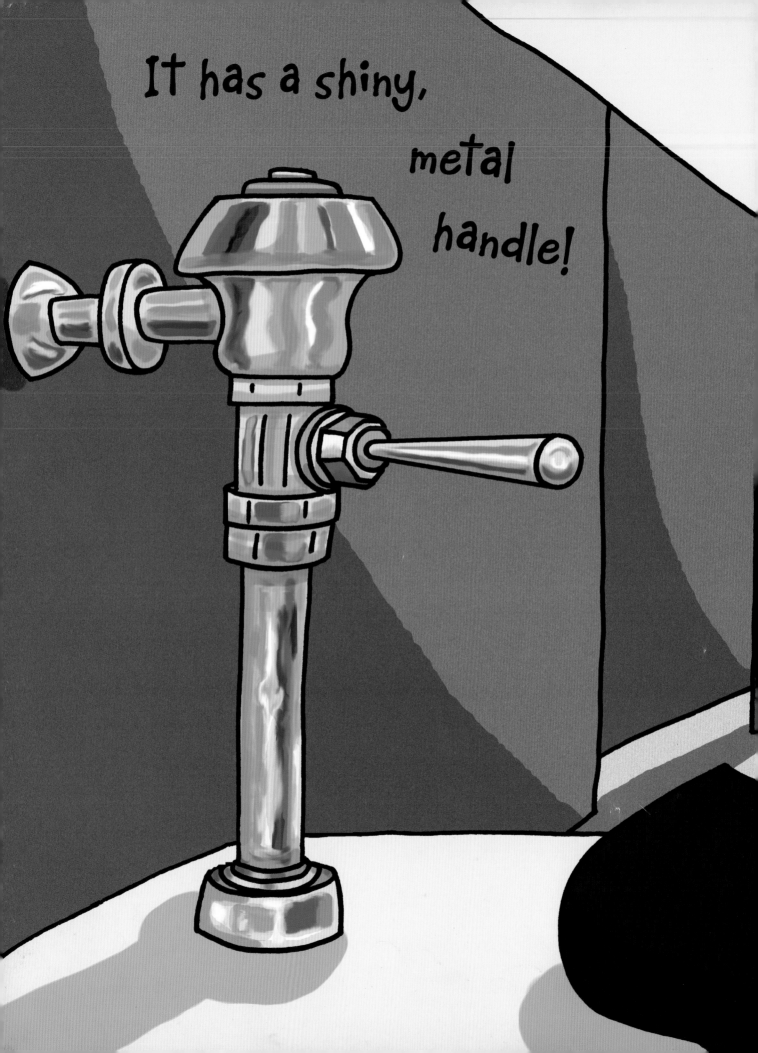

That big, loud flush
makes me afraid
that it might suck me down!

I think that toilet is **haunted!**

...and now I'm too scared to wee!

Then when you are leaving and the flush is next to do,

you wave

and dance

and wiggle,

FLUSH! FLUUSH!

but the eye just stares at you.

From
high tank
toilets,

to
high tech
toilets,

Ah, but the funniest toilet is in the new

Duh End!